A Ma...

Steel Bridge

N
W E
S

River

The Field

Gas Bridge

Footpath

River

Towpath

The Canal

Jeremy Vole's house

Ducks

To Osney Lock

Water Meadow

Presented to

Oliver Wale

St Matthew's

Sunday Funday Club

1998-99

CHRISTIAN ART–KINGSWAY COMMUNICATIONS LTD.,
EASTBOURNE 01323 437700

Riverbank Stories
-TWO-

The Tale of
Timothy Mallard

Stephen Lawhead

A LION BOOK
Oxford · Batavia · Sydney

Copyright © 1990 Stephen Lawhead
Illustrations copyright © 1990 Laura Potter

Published by
Lion Publishing plc
Sandy Lane West, Oxford, England
ISBN 0 7459 2116 7
Albatross Books Pty Ltd
PO Box 320, Sutherland, NSW 2232, Australia
ISBN 0 7324 0570 X

First edition 1990
First paperback edition 1992
Reprinted 1993

A catalogue record for this book is available
from the British Library

Printed and bound in Great Britain by
Cox & Wyman, Reading

CONTENTS

1

A Bad Egg

Right from the moment he poked his fluffy little head out the egg, Timothy Mallard knew that something had gone wrong. Call it a hunch, call it a lucky guess. The duckling didn't know what it was, but he knew that something had gone amiss.

And he was right.

Too bad for Timothy. Because the thing that was not quite right was *him*!

His mother was there to welcome him into the world – along with his eight brothers. Little Timothy shook the last bit of eggshell from his tail and quacked his first quack. "Greetings!" he said. Then he looked around the big, feather-lined nest at his family, who were all staring at him rather strangely.

"What is it?" he quacked. "What's everybody looking at?"

"You're funny!" said Brother Number One.

"Shhh!" hushed his mother quickly. "Hello, Timothy," she said, gathering him under her wing. "How do you feel, darling?"

"Great!" cheeped Timothy. "What's for lunch?"

"Hey, everybody!" cried Brother Number Two. "Look at Timothy!"

"What!" Timothy quacked again, beginning to feel that something was very wrong indeed, and that the something had *something* to do with him.

"It's . . . er, nothing, my dear," said Mrs Mallard. "How about a swim?"

"Great!" replied Timothy. And his eight brothers began to laugh. "What?" he wondered, growing worried.

"You're *white!*" cried Brother Number Three. And they all began to laugh again, shouting, "Whitey! Whitey! Whitey!"

It was true. Instead of the snazzy black-brown-and-yellow stripes of his brothers' handsome coats, Timothy's coat was white. And not a little speckle-here-speckle-there sort of white, either. His coat was a bright, spotless white all over. Like a snowdrift, or a bowl of milk – through-and-through white. Gleaming white like a new tennis ball.

"Yipes!" yelled Timothy. "I'm white!"

It is always a very great shock for any creature to discover that he is different from his fellows, and Timothy was no exception. So he did what any creature would do in his position: he fell down in a fluffy heap and began to cry.

"There, there, now. Don't cry." His mother stroked his back with a wing-tip and tried to comfort him. "It's all right, Timothy. I'm sūre you'll grow out of it. They're only baby feathers after all."

"Whitey! Whitey! You're not righty!" cheeped his eight brothers gleefully. They began jumping up and down, and singing this song.

"Stop it!" quacked Mrs Mallard. "It isn't polite to make fun of the unfortunate. Besides, he's your brother and you must be nice to him."

"We can't help it," shouted Brother Number Four. "He's a bad egg!" And they all began to laugh again. "Bad egg! Bad egg!"

"Just wait till your father gets home," warned the mother duck. "He'll soon sort you out!"

Unfortunately, Timothy's father was not as much help as he might have been. Malcolm Mallard took one look at his son and said, "The lads are right, dear. The boy is white."

"I know, Mal," replied Mrs Mallard, "but he *is* your son."

"Well, we could paint him, I suppose."

"Don't be silly."

"What do you want me to do, Meryl?"

"Speak to the boy, Malcolm," replied the mother duck. "Look at him – he's taking it hard. He feels terrible. See if you can perk him up a bit."

"I'll do my best, love." The big drake waddled over to where Timothy sat in a miserable lump, his little yellow bill resting on his snowy white chest. "Well, well, Timothy," he said. "Welcome to the family, son."

The unhappy duckling raised his head and looked at his father's brilliant coat. It was green and grey and maroon and black – a whole rainbow! Timothy had never seen anything so beautiful. "Gosh!" he gasped.

"Your mum tells me you're feeling a bit down in the beak, son. What's the problem, then?"

Timothy sniffed back a tear and dabbed at his eye with a stubby wing. His head flopped down again.

"Come on," coaxed the drake, "why not tell your old dad? What's the matter, boy-o?"

"I'm white," sighed Timothy. "I'm very, very white."

"But that's not the end of the world, is it? 'Course not! There are worse things."

"Like what?"

"Well, I mean, things like . . ." The big mallard thought for a moment. "Well, all sorts of things really – I mean, there must be. Lots of things. It numbs the brain to think of them all."

"Like what?" Timothy wanted to know. "What could possibly be worse?"

"Oh, well . . . you might have been a goose," said his father at last. "Or a grebe. You wouldn't want to be a grebe, would you? Or a widgeon? 'Course not! A mallard – that's the thing! Right?"

"I suppose so," sniffed the unhappy duckling.

"So there you are. You've just got to buck up," father duck told him. "Life deals you a lemon, son, you make lemonade. Am I right? 'Course I'm right. Now give us a smile. There's a good lad." The big drake patted his son on the head and sent him off with his brothers for a swimming lesson.

"Well?" asked the mother duck. "How did it go?"

"Smashing," replied Malcolm. "Terrific lad, once you get to know him. I think he'll see things differently from now on."

"That's good, dear." The mother duck watched her ducklings skitter off across the water, dodging among the reeds and rushes. With their mottled coats, all the other ducklings disappeared into the dappled shadows. But one duck shone like a little white light bulb. "Oh dear," his mother sighed. "He'll take a deal of watching."

"Never you worry, Meryl," said Malcolm Mallard. "No son of mine was ever a bad egg. Old Tim'll turn out all right. Just you wait and see."

The mother duck slipped into the water to chase after her brood. "I just hope he gets the chance to turn out at all," she said as she paddled off. "Life can be hard for a mallard born white."

2

Hardly a Prayer

It was spring in Riverbank. The winter was over and the warm rains had done their work. There were blooms blooming and buds budding everywhere. New sprouts were sprouting and green grass growing. What with all the blooming and budding, sprouting and growing, it was a very busy place indeed.

All the creatures of Riverbank were just as busy with their nests and burrows. The annual spring clean was in full swing. The ducks, swans and moorhens were either waiting for their egglings to hatch, or were scurrying around to find enough food for their hungry broods. Just keeping everyone fed was a full-time sunrise-to-sunset job.

Every morning Mrs Mallard and her children left the big, feather-lined nest among the long rushes of the canal below the Gas Bridge and

swam out in search of food. Mother Duck swam leisurely along, pausing to up-end now and then for a choice bit of water violet. The ducklings darted here and there, skittering across the water like fuzzy little dodgem boats.

While Mother Mallard sampled the delicate spring cresses, the ducklings bobbed for midges – a game played by popping straight up out of the water to snatch one of the tiny black nuisances out of the air and gulp it down. Great fun!

The ducklings thought this a fine sport, and held competitions among themselves to see who could catch and eat the most midges. Timothy, desperate to show his brothers that he was good for something, worked long and hard, and got very good at the game. He could grab a midge on the wing quicker than any of the others, and he won the competitions – which he thought would make his brothers like him better.

But instead it only made them cross.

"Who does he think he is?" they muttered to themselves. "Little Mister Know-it-All! He thinks he's so special. We'll show him! Just wait and see if we don't!"

Most of the time, Timothy was so busy learning about the great wide world around him that he quite forgot that he was different – until someone reminded him. Usually it went like this:

There they'd all be, swimming along nice as you please, watching the riverbank slide by ever so pleasantly. And then they'd bump into someone they hadn't met before.

"A very nice brood, Meryl," the stranger would say. "A fine brood indeed . . . *Oh, dear!*"

The *Oh, dear* was Timothy.

He would dart under his mother's wing where no one could see him, and he'd stay there until it was safe to come out. Then Mother Mallard would comfort him. "There, there!" she'd say. "It's all right. Pay it no mind. I like you just the way you are."

"Look at him," grumbled his brothers. "He causes all the trouble, and *he's* the one who gets all the sympathy."

The ducklings did not understand that Timothy needed the sympathy and protection of his mother much more than they did. Because a little white duck is like a white flag. Everyone notices – friend and foe alike. When trouble comes, a white duck cannot simply vanish into the shadows like his brothers; he is a constant danger to himself. So Mrs Mallard had to take special care of Timothy, giving him extra love and attention.

The other ducklings saw this and it made them hate Timothy all the more.

"He makes me sick," said Brother Number Five. "It's embarrassing," replied Brother Number Six. "Humiliating!" added Brother Number Seven. "Disgraceful!" quacked Brother Number Eight.

"I have an idea," said Brother Number One. "We'll give him a lesson he'll never forget."

"Yes, let's get him!" said Brother Number Four.

"We'll show him he's not so special!" said the others, and from that moment they began plotting how to get rid of Timothy.

The next day, when the ducks went out for their morning ramble, they ran into another brood of mallards – a family of seven from up the river. And the two mother ducks began talking, as ducks will do, leaving the children to scamper around and play by themselves.

"Psst! This is it," whispered Brother Number One to Brother Number Two. "Pass the word." And the word was passed from one to the next down the line. All except for Timothy, of course. He was not to know what was about to happen.

The new ducklings whispered and pointed at Timothy; some of them laughed. "Look at that!" said Brother Number One loudly. "Are we going to let them make fun of our brother?"

"What?" wondered Timothy, who had never heard any of his brothers so much as whisper a kind word to him before.

Number One Brother paddled up and put his wing around Timothy's shoulder. "Stop laughing at our brother," he told the rude ducklings. "You may not know it, but Timothy here is the world champion at bobbing for midges."

"Go on," said the other ducklings. "He's *white*! He's a freak!"

"That may be. But he's still the best midge catcher you ever saw," said Timothy's brother proudly.

"We'll prove it to you," said the others.

Timothy was pleased and surprised to hear his brothers talk this way about him. He felt his heart swell up with pride. I *am* worth something after all, he thought.

"Show them, Timothy," his brother told him. The other brothers gathered around him, shouting, "Yes! Yes! Show them, Timothy! Show them!"

Well, Timothy was so happy to hear this high praise from his brothers that he began bobbing for midges right then and there. He jumped higher and faster than he'd ever jumped before. He leaped and he bounced and he caught midges two and three and four at a time.

Very soon he'd caught all the midges nearby, but his brothers urged him on. "Look! Over there, Timothy – there's some more! Go get 'em!"

And off he went. His brothers cheered. The more he caught, the louder they shouted. When he ran out of midges they spied some more and sent him after them. Timothy was so dizzy with showing off, he did not notice that the cheers were getting farther and farther away.

After a while Timothy became tired of hopping and bopping, and stopped. He turned round and discovered that he was all alone in a strange part of Riverbank. "Hey!" he called. "Where *is* everybody?"

There was no answer. They were gone.

Uh-oh, thought Timothy, and he felt a sinking feeling in the pit of his stomach. I'm in trouble now. *Big* trouble.

Timothy didn't know the half of it. It was bad enough to be a white mallard duckling; now he was a *lost* white mallard duckling, and that made it a million times worse. Little lost ducklings, sad to say, do not usually last long on their own. And little lost *white* mallard ducklings have hardly a prayer.

3

Sold up the River

Timothy had only one slender hope of survival: find his family as quickly as possible. So, wasting not a moment, he scooted off, his feet churning water like little egg-beaters.

He raced here and there, searching among the reeds and rushes for his mother and brothers. He quacked his best "Help! I'm lost!" quack until he thought his bill would fall off. No one heard him. No one came to his rescue.

Once he thought he saw his family cruising along in the distance and he skittered off to join them. "Whew!" he thought. "At last!" But no sooner had he taken his place at the end of the line, than the mother duck turned and saw him. "White!" she screamed. "Out! Out! Away! Get away from my ducklings!"

The Mallard-who-wasn't-Mum flew at him and thumped him with her wings. She hissed and snapped at him with her bill, and nibbled his head. "Ow!" the duckling cried. The strange duck raised such a fuss, with all her snapping and hissing and nibbling, that poor Timothy had no choice but to flee for his little white life.

"Mamma!" he cried, the tears rolling from his eyes and down his fluffy cheeks. "I'm lost! Help me, Mamma!"

Frantic with fear, Timothy began swimming madly along the riverbank, calling out as he went. He saw a black moorhen poking among the reeds along the shore. He dashed to her. "Please, help me. I'm lost," he cried. "Have you seen my mother?"

The moorhen looked at him oddly. "Who are you, child?"

"Timothy Mallard," he answered, sniffing back the tears.

"Well, I never," clucked the moorhen, shaking her head in amazement. "A white mallard!"

"Please," wailed Timothy. "I'm lost. Can you help me?"

"Let me see," said the moorhen. "I don't recall any *white* mallards. I'm sure I would remember if I'd ever seen any."

"But *they're* not white," said Timothy. "It's only me that's white."

"Is that so?" wondered the moorhen. "Think of that."

"My father's name is Malcolm," the duckling explained."Do you know him?"

The moorhen shook her head. "I can't really say – there are so many mallards, you see. All flocking together. It's hard to tell them apart, don't you know." The little lost duckling began crying once again and the moorhen felt sorry for him. "But I know what you might do."

"Yes?" Timothy's tears stopped instantly. "I'll do anything."

"Well, you might try going further up-river. There are some more mallards up-river, and I'm sure you would find someone who could tell you where you belong."

"Up-river?" the duckling wondered doubtfully.

"Not far, mind. Just a short way. If you keep going, you'll find them."

Terrific! thought Timothy. If I hurry, I'll just be in time for supper. And he hurried away as fast as his little webbed feet could flap.

It was difficult swimming upstream against the current. Timothy had to stop and rest along the way. He did not know how far he went, but the duckling saw no other ducks or birds, no nests at all – just the blank face of a river-wall.

He was solidly lost. That was bad enough. Far worse was the fact that the farther up-river he went, the more lost he became. The more lost he became, the more certain he was that he had been sold up the river by his brothers.

So he turned around and began swimming down-river instead. He really did not know what else to do. Besides, it was much easier drifting with the current than swimming against it. He chugged along, keeping close to the bank, cheeping a little worried cheep every now and then, just in case anyone heard him.

Eventually, someone did . . . Mrs Smith's very fat yellow-spotted cat named Boris.

4

Cat Snacks

Quite a number of cats lived along the banks of River. All sorts of cats. Most of them kept to themselves like good cats. But Boris was *not* a good cat. He was one cat who made it his business to cause as much trouble as possible for anyone who happened across his path.

Maybe his blotchy yellow fur made him cross. Maybe he always climbed out of his cat-flap on the wrong side. Maybe he'd had his fat tail trodden on as a kitten and never got over it. Whatever it was, it made him quarrelsome and cruel. Then again, big bruisers like Boris need little enough excuse to throw their weight around. He just liked being bad.

He *enjoyed* beating up lesser creatures. He liked catching mice and birds. He liked slapping fish. Whenever he could get hold of something small and helpless in his sharp claws, bad old Boris was one happy cat.

All the other pets along the river knew one thing if they knew anything at all: Boris was the cruelest cat in Riverbank. Pound for pound – and Boris had plenty of pounds – there was not a nastier cat to be found anywhere. Pure spite with fat yellow spots!

Boris liked to sit on the very edge of the towpath at the top of the steps leading down to the river; he'd sit there and close his eyes and dream up new ways to make trouble. Every now and then he'd open one eye and peer around to see if anything interesting was coming his way. By "interesting," he meant anything weak and small.

As it happened, little Timothy came paddling by at just the moment old Boris opened that mean green eye of his. "Hmmm," thought Boris to himself, "what have we here? Too late for breakfast, too early for dinner . . . Must be brunch."

Timothy saw the cat at nearly the same instant the cat saw him. But since he had never seen a cat before, the duckling didn't understand the danger he was in. So he gave his quivery quack and said, "I'm lost!"

"What's that?" Boris said. "I don't think I heard you."

Timothy looked and saw that there were some steps leading from the water to the towpath. The first step was just under the water, so he swam to it and stood up. "Please, sir," the duckling said loudly, "I'm lost. Can you help me find my way home?"

Bad old Boris stretched his fat legs and stood up slowly. "Sorry," he said, "I'm not getting this at all. You say you want to find a pay phone?"

"No – a way home," Timothy shouted. "I've lost my mother."

"Tossed your butter?" wondered the cat. "That can't be right. Can you speak a little louder?"

"I don't think so," the duckling said, and he started to cry.

"Hold on," said Boris. "I'll come down and we'll get this cleared up in a trice."

The fat cat eased his bulk down the stairs. Blump! Blump! Blump! "Don't cry little fellow," soothed the cat as he came nearer. "Old Boris will see you right . . . or know the reason why."

He already knew the reason why, the cruel thing. But poor little Timothy did not know it. The cat stalked down the stone steps to where the duckling stood in the water, and settled himself one stair-step away.

"What a pretty little morsel you ar-r-re," purred the cat. "So fresh and white you ar-r-re."

Little Timothy heard something in the cat's silky purr that warned him. He stopped crying instantly.

"That's better," said Boris slyly. "I was just now thinking about having a wee snack. Could I interest you in a bite?"

Before Timothy could answer, the bad cat's claws were out and his paws were tight around the duckling's neck. "QUAWCK!" screamed Timothy. "HEL-L-L-P!"

"SHHH," soothed the cat. "Don't let's make a fuss. Didn't I say old Boris would see you right? – Right into my mouth!"

Timothy struggled in the cat's paws, but the more he twisted this way and that, the more the cat's claws tightened around him. He was caught. He was trapped. He was a cat snack, and no two ways about it!

Fun and Games

Boris eyed his snack greedily. "Such a tasty morsel," he said, green eyes gleaming. "Such a toothsome bite."

"Please!" cried Timothy. "Don't eat me!"

"Oh, I'm not going to eat you, Duckie!" said Boris. "At least, not right away. I like to have a little fun first. I thought we might play a game. Fun and games, Duckie – yes?"

Timothy did not like the sound of that. He could feel the cat's claws digging into him. They hurt. "Please," he whimpered, "let me go."

"All right," replied the cat with an evil grin. "You can go."

Boris opened his paws and let go. Timothy fell back into the water with a splash. "Oops! Sorry. Here, let me help you," said Boris. With a swipe, he reached down and scooped Timothy out of the water again, and threw him up on to the dry step.

"I thought ducks *liked* water," he said. "But no matter. Let's get you dried off."

The cat began to bat the duckling back and forth between his paws, smacking him to and fro like a shuttlecock. Battered, dizzy, scared beyond words, little Timothy was helpless against the big fat baddy. He struggled, he cheeped for help, he scrambled and rolled and bounced on the hard stone step – flat on his back one moment, head over tail-feathers the next. The duckling didn't know which end was up.

Boris grinned his wicked grin all the while. He had played this game lots of times. He dearly loved it, the black-hearted old darling. The game always ended when he finally got tired of torturing his prey and gulped it down.

"You know," the cat said, "I had hoped you would put up more of a fight – make the game a bit more interesting." He yawned, showing his fine sharp teeth. "But I fear I am getting bored. And when I get bored, I get hungry. In fact, I think I feel a trifle peckish r-i-g-h-t . . . NOW!"

Boris flicked his paw and flung the duckling toward him. The bad cat opened his mouth wide. Timothy saw the sharp teeth and the pink tongue – and he beat his fuzzy, featherless wings with all his might. SNAP! The cat teeth snapped like a trap.

Bad old Boris was so sure of himself – and so lazy – that he forgot how quick frightened ducklings can be. And Timothy was frightened half out of his fuzz. He beat his tiny wings and skittered across the step. Boris felt his teeth snap shut on thin air. "Oi!"

Timothy reached the edge of the step and flopped down on his belly. Boris slapped his paw down on the duckling's back. SPLAT! "Leaving so soon, Duckie?" the cat said. "Oh, we're not finished yet."

The helpless duckling felt Boris's claws sharp on his back. He gathered his little webbed feet and squeezed out from under the paw, leaving a bunch of white fluff behind. Then he was over the edge of the step and diving head first into the river.

Boris did not like to see his snack getting away from him and made a last swipe and grab with his paws. But the fat cat reached too far, his great weight tilted, and he fell off the step and into the river. KEER-PLOOSH!

Bad Boris went under and came up spitting and hissing. Oh, he was vexed! He dragged himself out of the water and stood on the step dripping and sputtering and looking like a soggy sack of lemon jelly.

Timothy Mallard hit the water running. He skittered right across the river and didn't stop until he was on the other side, and far away from the nasty cat.

Boris shook himself and then put his tail in the air, as if to say, "I meant to do that." He heaved himself slowly up the stone steps and back to his place on the wall where he could dry out and dream up some more of his fiendish schemes.

By the time Timothy stopped running he was very far away from that bad old Boris. Yes, and he was farther away from home than ever, too.

"Woe is me!" he wailed. "I don't think I'll ever get home again."

This was exactly what his wicked brothers had in mind, of course. They hoped never to see him again, and they did not care a June bug what happened to him. They thought themselves very clever ducks to have tricked him so easily.

Timothy tried not to think about that. All he cared about right now was a soft nest and a bite to eat. He found a hideaway among the weeds against the river wall and ate a few midges. They didn't help fill him up very much, but he was too tired to hunt for anything else. And too scared to go hunting anyway. He'd been separated from his family, lost, nibbled by an angry duck, and mugged by a cat. He felt he'd had more than his share of fun and games for one day.

6

A Long, Cold Night

Timothy had never spent a night alone . . . outside his nest . . . in the cold . . . and dark . . . all by himself . . . Oooh!

As the sun went down, the shadows stretched long. The little duckling began to miss his nest and his family. Being crowded together under his mother's wing made him feel safe, not to mention warm. He was not warm now. He was cold and lonely. And sore.

Night darkened the riverbank world and made it a strange and frightening place. The shadows deepened. A thin, ghostly white mist rose and snaked along the water. Timothy shivered in his little hide-out in the weeds.

He heard noises: long, shaky C-R-E-A-K-S, and loud POP-POP-POPS! Low GURGLE-URGLE-URGLES, high SCRE-E-E-CHES, and doleful SIGH-IGHS-IGHS. He heard moans, groans and whispers, whimpers, mewls, grunts, bawls and shrieks.

The little duckling listened to this weird symphony and shivered all the more. The night was one big, frightening racket. Where did all these awful sounds come from? What made them?

No, better not to know. It was scary enough having to listen to the noises, without knowing how they were made. Timothy huddled in the weeds and tried not to think about the frightening sounds. He tried not to think about how hungry he was. Or how cold. Or how lonely.

But the more he tried not to think about those things, the more he could think of nothing else. And the long, cold, hungry, lonely, frightening night became even longer and colder and hungrier, lonelier and more frightening, for thinking about it.

He wondered what his family was doing. Did they miss him? Were they worried about him? Were they searching for him? Or were they curled up in the nest, all warm and safe and fed . . . It was no use. Try as he might he always came back to the same place: he was alone and afraid, with no hope of ever seeing his family again. And that made him feel worse than ever.

Timothy tucked his bill under his little wing and curled himself into a small, miserable ball. He closed his eyes, but he did not sleep. He was much too frightened to sleep. He just stayed huddled in his hiding spot, a pitiful, shivering little knot of fluff. And the long, cold night stretched on and on and on . . .

Meeting a Monster!

The next morning, as soon as it was light enough to see, Timothy left his hiding-place. The morning mist rolled thick on the water as he headed down-river in search of his family.

He was so hungry he no longer knew where he was going. He no longer cared. He decided just to go with the flow, and see where River took him. Up ahead he saw a bridge – but it wasn't the bridge he knew. It was bigger and made of steel. In fact, everywhere he looked, everything was big and strange and hard-looking.

Gone were the reeds and rushes, the nests and burrows and the cool, hidden, shady places. The moss and mud of the riverbank gave way to stone banks. And instead of the green grass and trees of Water Meadow, all he saw was concrete and stone houses.

"Mamma!" he cried, as he paddled along. "Mamma! Mamma! Mamma!"

"STROKE!" came the answer.

"Mamma!"

"STROKE!"

Suddenly, out of the mist, rushed a terrible thing. A monster! Sleek and long and smooth, with four flailing flipper arms on each side and eight humps down the middle, and a great, sharp beak slicing the water – it almost flew over the river, croaking its horrible cry as it came: STROKE! STROKE! STROKE!

It was fast – too fast for Timothy. He turned and ran, his feet hardly touching the water. But the terrible monster caught him and gathered him in.

Timothy was lifted up, dashed against the monster's hard shell and thrown aside. The next thing Timothy knew, he was tangled among the monster's rippling arms. CHOP! SPLASH! STROKE!

The duckling was pulled down in a whirlpool made by one of the long, slashing arms. He spun round and round and came popping up like a cork. "Help!" he cried. CHOP! SPLASH! STROKE! The monster rushed on.

Dazed and confused, Timothy stared after the frightening thing. Whatever it was, the humpy-

backed monster was not the least bit interested in him. It did not slow down or turn round, but kept right on going until it disappeared into the mist, taking its strange call of STROKE! STROKE! with it.

The duckling shook himself dry and continued on toward the bridge, staying close to the wall in case the monster came back. He took up his forlorn cry once more. "Mamma! Mamma!" he quacked, listening for an answering call. "Mamma! Where are you?"

There is not a more pitiful sight anywhere than a poor little lost duckling looking for its mother. Pitiful and *tempting*. Sad but true. Because, believe it or not, there are creatures in the river that make bad old Boris look like a boy scout.

Unhappily, one of those creatures heard little Timothy's mournful cry and answered it.

8

Spike

Timothy came to the big steel bridge. It was dark under the bridge. The water was cool in the shadows. This is where the creature waited – down in the cool shadowy depths. Watching . . . waiting . . . until some unsuspecting thing wandered near. Then –

– up from the dark depths of the river the cold thing would streak. Like a torpedo! Like a rocket!

The duckling had no warning. One moment he was simply paddling along, sweet as you please. The next moment, WHOOSH! He was flying up out of the water and spinning through the air.

Timothy didn't know what hit him. He saw a great green, scaly side, and a huge red eye. He saw a vast, gaping mouth and row upon row of teeth sharp as needles. He kicked his feet and squirmed to get away.

CHOMP! The thing caught hold of his leg, and then down it plunged. SPLASH!

Timothy was yanked under water. Deeper and deeper the creature dived, his powerful jaws firmly clamped on the duckling's skinny little leg. "Help! Save me!" Timothy cried. But he was under water so his cry came out as no more than a thin, bubbly gargle.

The creature was taking him down to its lair among the rocks under the bridge. There it would, without a doubt, gobble him down. It would have eaten him already but for Timothy's kicking and squirming.

No matter, the fearful creature was nothing if not patient. It could wait days for its prey to swim along, so it could certainly wait another moment or two for a meal as tasty as Timothy – but first it had to get a better grip on its duckling dinner.

The cold creature opened its mouth slightly.

That was all Timothy needed. He felt the jaws loosen and he kicked with all his might. A duckling's might is not much, but sometimes even a little is enough.

Quick as a blink, Timothy was streaking to the surface. The hateful creature was startled by this escape; it was not used to having its meals get away. It paused to think what had happened.

This moment's hesitation was all the duckling needed. Timothy not only reached the surface, but had time to scream, "Help! Someone save me!"

The nasty creature raced up and after Timothy in a flash. But the duckling was scared, and fear made him quick. Timothy did not wait to be caught again. He skittered over the water like a pebble launched from a sling-shot.

The creature broke water right behind, missing Timothy by the merest fraction of a feather. The duckling did not look back. He flapped his stubby wings and flittered this way and that in a helpless, hopeless flight, squawking all the way. "Help! Save me! Somebody! Help!"

The duckling was so frightened, and so frantic to get away, that he was not watching where he was going. He dived and dodged and – PLOOF! – ran smack dab into a towering wall – a wall of . . . white feathers?

Yes. It was a swan.

Timothy looked up and saw the long, snaking neck coiled high above him, ready to strike. Yie!

With a yelp the duckling back-paddled on the water. But too late. The swan hissed. Timothy threw his wings over his head. ZING! The swan struck.

Timothy did not feel a thing. He peeked out just in time to see the swan's sturdy bill strike the awful green creature square on top of its scaly head as it leaped from the water. The creature's jaws snapped shut with a sound like a rat trap springing closed, and the horrid green thing fell back into the river with a tremendous splash.

The water grew silent again. The waves turned back into ripples and flowed away. All was calm and peaceful again. A wet and trembling Timothy looked up to find the swan staring sternly at him.

"Wh-where'd y-you come f-from?" the frightened mallard asked.

"Oh, I'm always around," answered the swan. "Lucky for you, I might add. Are you hurt, hatchling?"

"I – I don't th-think so," Timothy stammered.

"Didn't anyone ever tell you that it's dangerous playing around bridges?"

"No," Timothy admitted.

"Well, it is. Very dangerous," the swan said with a scolding clack with his bill. "Though I don't suppose I need to tell you that now."

Timothy shivered, thinking about what almost happened to him. "That horrible creature – what was it?"

"That was Spike. He is a pike – a more dangerous fish you never want to meet." The swan regarded the duck closely. "What, may I ask, are you? Not a swan, surely?"

"I'm a mallard – Malcolm and Meryl's eggling."

"A white mallard," mused the swan. "What won't they think of next?" He ruffled his feathers and spread his wings wide. "My name's Big Sam. What's yours?"

"I'm Timothy."

"Good. Now then, where's your brood?"

Timothy hung his head. "I don't know. I'm lost," he sniffed.

"Well, are you an up-river duck, or a down-river duck?"

"I don't know."

"And I don't suppose you know where you are now?"

"No," moaned Timothy miserably. "I don't know *anything*."

"Thought as much," the swan said. "Well, you can't stay here. Spike has a short memory. He'll soon forget about the nip I've just given him. You'd best move on before he comes back."

"But I don't have anywhere to go!" the duckling whimpered. Tears filled his eyes and he began to sniffle again.

"All right, all right. Turn off the waterworks, sport. Big Sam knows a trick or two. It just so happens I know a place where you can get a crust and a bed."

"You do?" the duckling sniffed. "Where?"

"Not far from here," Big Sam told him. "Come on. If you can keep up, I'll show you." The swan moved off slowly, and Timothy hurried after him.

9

The Boatlady

The big white swan and his little white shadow continued on down the river and Timothy saw that everything was made of stone: the houses, the riverbank, the towpath. He saw a bridge and that was made of stone as well. It was big and busy.

"That's Folly Bridge," Big Sam told him.

"Why's it called the Folly?"

"That, my little fluffy friend, you will quickly discover if you ever try to cross it."

"Oh," replied Timothy, looking at all the buses, bikes, and cars zooming across the busy bridge, "I don't think I'd ever want to cross it."

"Good man."

They swam on and passed under the Folly. Timothy stayed close to Big Sam in case there were any more hungry pike lurking in the dark depths beneath the bridge. But nothing came shooting up out of the water and they passed through safely.

Once on the other side, Timothy thought he must have entered different world. There were trees once more, and a meadow – by far the biggest meadow the duckling had ever seen – with grass growing right down to the water's edge. Gone was the harsh world of steel and stone and concrete.

"That's the *Head of the River*," said Big Sam as they swam by a large building. "You'll get some of your best meals there. But not now. It's too early in the season. Give it a few weeks though, and the tourists will start flocking."

Timothy did not understand what Big Sam said about seasons, and had not the least idea what kind of bird a *tourist* might be. But he nodded politely and they swam on. Behind the *Head of the River* was a small boat-house with a little jetty and a dozen or so punts and rowing boats tied to the wooden planks. On this jetty stood a woman in a pink-flowered dress. She had big friendly smile, and a bag of dry bread in her hand. She was actually throwing the bread in the water and – Timothy could not believe his eyes! – feeding a whole flock of noisy ducks and sea-gulls. Astounding!

"That's the Boatlady," Big Sam told the duckling. "She runs the boat hire. And every day about this time she brings the bread," the swan explained, and curled his neck grandly. "What do you say, hatchling? Will that do you?"

"Yes, please!"

"Then what are you waiting for? Scoot! Or you'll get left out!"

Timothy hesitated. "Aren't you coming?"

"Not today. Another time, perhaps. I'm on my way down-river."

"You're leaving me?"

"Don't worry. The Boatlady will take care of you. Just stay close to the jetty and don't let any of those gulls give you a bad time. You'll be right as rain."

"Couldn't you stay just a little while?" cried Timothy.

"I'm always passing by," replied the swan. "I'll probably pop in again one of these days and surprise you." Big Sam turned, arched his wings and, like a ship unfurling its sails, began gliding slowly away. "Goodbye, Fluffball."

"Goodbye, Big Sam. And thanks!"

Timothy watched the swan swim away and then remembered what he'd said about getting

left out. So he hurried over to the jetty and joined the mass of ducks diving for bread.

The bread came down, and he dived for it. But, try as he might, Timothy could not get a bite. The other ducks were bigger, and the gulls were quicker. Timothy dodged this way and that, but always someone else gobbled down the bread before he could get to it.

"Such manners! Hasn't anyone ever heard of sharing?" he wondered. "I'll starve to death before any of these birds gives me a chance. There's only one thing to do," he decided, and an idea popped into his head.

It was bold. It was brave. It was daring. It was the only thing he could think of.

Timothy left the swarming mob of waterfowl and paddled round to the other side of the jetty to where the boats were tied. The jetty was too high to hop up on – too high for an ordinary duckling, that is. Timothy, because he was a champion hopper, thought he just might make it if he tried really hard.

Scrunching himself up into a ball, he crouched, then up he popped. HOP!

Missed. He crouched again and . . . HOP! It was more difficult than bobbing for midges, but not much different. He crouched again . . . HOP!

HOP! HOP!

He was getting tired. No food, no sleep, fighting with Spike – not to mention Boris and the humpy-backed monster – had used up all his energy. He had come to the end of his small strength at last.

Well, maybe he had enough oomph for just one more jump. He eyed the edge of the jetty, scrunched up . . . HOP!

Made it! He scrambled up, waddled happily over to the Boatlady and introduced himself with a cheery cheep. The Boatlady looked down and saw the little white duck standing at her feet. "Well, well, what have we here?"

Timothy cheeped again and fluffed up his white fuzz, as he'd seen Big Sam do, to make himself look important – or at least not quite so small and bedraggled.

The Boatlady smiled. "Cheeky little thing, you are. Where'd you come from, love?" The duckling cheeped loudly. "Are you hungry, dearie?"

She put her hand down and Timothy saw a nice big piece of bread. He stepped nearer, but was too tired to reach out and take the food. Instead, he stretched out his neck and rested his bill on her palm. "Fancy that," she said. "You're fair done in, you are."

The Boatlady scooped Timothy up and held him in her hands. She looked at him closely, and then looked at him again. "Do I believe my eyes? Look at this! Albert!" she called. "Albert, look what we've got here – a white duck!"

The woman carried the duckling to the boathouse, where a man sat in a chair by the door reading a newspaper.

"There's nothing unusual about a white duck, Bea," the man said without looking up. "That's common for ducks, white is."

"Not for mallards, it isn't."

"Then it isn't a mallard, Bea."

"Yes it is. Just have a look and see for yourself, Mr Know-So-Much."

She held the duckling under his nose and the man lowered his newspaper. He glanced at Timothy – then took a longer look, and then he squinted one eye, cocked his head to the side, and studied the duckling closely. He noted the delicate markings, the bill and the shape of the feet. "That there's a white mallard, Bea," Albert said at last.

"So what have I been telling you?"

"What's a white mallard doing here?"

"He marched up to me while I was feeding the free-loaders. I think he's lost."

"Nonsense," said Albert. "Ducks don't get lost, Bea. Of course they don't. They live on the river, don't they. There's the river. How can he get lost?"

"I mean," insisted the Boatlady, "that he has misplaced his family."

"Driven off, more like." The man returned to his newspaper.

"Don't you be terrible, Albert." The Boatlady held the duckling next to her cheek. "Who would drive off a sweet little snowball like this?"

"Animals are peculiar, Bea. They don't tolerate differences the way we humans do. Very prejudiced, beasts are." Albert turned the page. "You'd best put him back."

"Put him back? I won't. You just said he was driven off. I expect they'll kill him next."

"That is as may be. But you can't keep a mallard duckling. They're born free, ducks are. They'll pine in captivity. Languish away and die. It says so in the *Times*."

"Well, if anybody would know about languishing, it would be you, Albert. You're a right expert on that subject. I say the little thing is lost, and I'm going to take care of him."

"You can't keep a wild duck, Bea. They'll turn on you every time."

"We'll see about that, Albert. Yes, we will," said the Boatlady firmly. "There's something special about this duckling – he's rare, and I mean to give him a fighting chance."

Freedom

Bea the Boatlady found a box for Timothy and made a nest for him out of shredded newspaper. She fed him warm milk with bits of toast. He gulped them down and promptly went to sleep. When he woke up, the Boatlady took him out and put him in a bucket she had filled with water from the river. Timothy had a swim and another snack. And then it was time to close up the boat hire for the night.

Albert chained the boats to the jetty and Bea put Timothy back in his box. She left some breadcrumbs and a dish of water for him. Then she carefully carried the box in the boat-house and left him there. "Good night, Duckie," she said. "I'll see you in the morning." Albert locked the door and Timothy was left alone.

It was odd sleeping in the boat-house. But it was quiet and, as long as he stayed in his box, pests like Boris and Spike could not get at him. He was safe.

But he was not happy. He thought about his family, and missed his mother and father. Timothy remembered his home on the riverbank and it broke his heart to think he would never see it, or his parents, ever again. He wasn't too sure about his brothers – they had treated him most cruelly. All the same, he cried himself to sleep that night, and more than a few nights after that.

Over the next few weeks Timothy grew very fond of Bea and Albert. They treated him kindly, and looked after him well. He lost his fluff and gained handsome white feathers, and grew big and strong on his diet of milk and toast. Sometimes the toast had a bit of jam left on it! Delicious! And he swam in the bucket every day, quacking endlessly, so that the Boatlady would know he liked his new home.

He did his best to forget all about the bad things that had happened to him, and to think only of his future with Bea and Albert at the boat hire and how much he liked it there. "I just want to stay here," he said to himself. "I belong here."

Then one day, as Bea filled the pail for his swim, Albert said, "He's getting too big for that bucket, Bea. It's time he was on his own."

Oh, no! thought Timothy. What will I do?

"Nonsense, Albert," chided Bea, picking up Timothy. She put him in the bucket as always, but frowned to see him.

"See?" said Albert. "He can hardly turn round in that thing."

"I'll just get a bigger bucket, then, Albert."

"You'll do no such thing, Bea. Turn him loose. If he was with his own kind, he'd be out of the nest by now."

The Boatlady bit her lip. "Well, if you say so, Albert. But I think he might get on better if we keep him a little longer – him being white and all."

"Turn him loose, Bea. It's the only way. It's sink or swim with ducks, you know. Sink or swim."

Bea sighed. "Perhaps you're right, Albert. But we can't just chuck the dear thing out – not after we've nursed him and kept him alive. Maybe we could ease him out gradual like."

"Have it your own way, Bea," replied Albert, turning the page of his newspaper. "Sometimes you've got to be cruel to be kind, you know."

The Boatlady picked Timothy up and carried him to the end of the jetty. "That's the River Thames," she told him. He knew that already, of course. "Be careful, it's a big unchancy world out there." *That* he knew already, as well. "I will leave your box on the jetty and you can come and go as you please. From now on, Duckie, you're a free bird."

Free! Timothy wasn't sure if he wanted to be free, but he liked the sound of it and thought it wouldn't hurt at least to give it a try. He could always come back to his box on the jetty if this freedom business didn't work out. So, when Bea tossed him gently into the air, he flapped his wings and flew off low across the water.

He landed in the middle of the river and quickly paddled back, quacking and quacking his pleasure. "Look!" he called to the Boatlady. "Look! I'm free! I'm swimming on my own! Look at me!"

Bea waved to him and called, "Come back whenever you like. You'll always have a place here."

Timothy quacked goodbye and paddled off to explore. His first stop was the *Head of the River*. He remembered what Big Sam the swan had told him about getting good meals there and decided to try it for himself. "I'm a free bird," he thought. "I'm going to have to learn these things if I'm to get on in the world."

The *Head of the River* had a restaurant with a

terrace overlooking the river. There were already a fair number of mallards and a few swans gathered in the water below the terraces, jostling one another for the few crumbs the people tossed to them. "This looks promising," he thought as he cruised up.

But the other ducks and swans took one look at him and set up a terrible racket. "Shove off, Whitey!" they cackled at him. "We don't need your kind hanging about! Get away!"

"I have just as much right as anyone," Timothy told them.

"Says who?" a smug young swan wanted to know. "You're a freak!"

"Go on, beat it!" shouted a loud-mouth mallard next to him. The duck took a swipe at Timothy with one of his wings. Another cried, "Freak!" and tried to nibble him. "Freak!"

There was little point in staying – the other ducks were bigger, and Timothy didn't feel like getting nibbled to bits for his trouble. Besides, he had a better idea. "All right," he told them, "I'm going. But you haven't seen the last of me!"

He swam slowly along the terrace. "Very well, they can keep the low road," he thought. "I'll take the high road."

With that he turned and . . . HOP! . . .jumped

right up on to the terrace above. A young boy saw him. "Hey! Did you see that?" he cried. "That white duck hopped straight out of the water. Here he comes!"

"Well, fancy that," said another, observing him closely. "I do believe it's a *white mallard*!"

Timothy fluffed up his feathers proudly and marched right into the midst of the crowd. "Pleased to meet you all," he quacked happily. "What's for lunch?"

The crowd on the terrace laughed and began tossing the choicest treats to Timothy: cucumber slices, sandwich crusts, potato crisps, and morsels of good yellow cheese. Timothy snatched them up at once. He had never tasted anything so good.

The other ducks stared at him with envy. "What's he doing up there? Showing off?"

"Showing off is right," said a young mallard. "He *is* the show, and he's stealing our crowd!"

It was true. Timothy was a hit. "This is easier than I thought," he said to himself. "I think freedom will suit me just fine."

11

One Famous Duck

The other ducks were too timid to go among humans but, thanks to Bea and Albert at the boat hire, Timothy was well used to people. He felt quite at ease. This easy confidence and his remarkable shade of white, odd as it was, made him an instant celebrity. Everywhere he went, it was the same story: "Look, Mum and Dad! What a funny duck! Can I give him my biscuit, Mum? Oh, please?"

Or: "Now there's something you don't see every day: a *white* mallard. Come here, little fellow, let's have a closer look. Care for a bit of lemon sponge?"

Timothy spent the whole afternoon entertaining people along the riverbank. Then, happy and full of food, he said goodbye to his new friends and swam back to the boat hire.

"What did I tell you, Albert?" said the Boatlady,

as Timothy hopped on to the jetty. "I told you he'd come back, and here he is."

The white mallard quacked a happy greeting, hopped into his box and settled down in his nest. That night he dreamed of chocolate biscuits, jam tarts, and cream-covered scones. He awoke the next morning so hungry that he set off at once to try his luck again. He swam first thing to the *Head of the River*, where he discovered that it wasn't opening time yet. So he found his way round to the back door, hopped up on the step and began quacking loudly.

In a moment the dark, curly head of the cook's helper thrust out and said, "'Ello, cheeky, what's up then?"

"I was just passing by, and thought I'd stop in," replied Timothy politely.

The cook's helper called to the cook. "Oi, Cook! See what we got 'ere – it's that white mallard I told you about."

A moment later the cook had joined his helper at the door. "So it is, Dennis. So it is." The cook leaned down and reached out a hand. "Hello there, Mr White Mallard. Care for a treat?"

Timothy gave the hand a friendly nibble. "Yes, please!"

"There's a rare bird, Dennis," said the cook.

"Fetch him a bit of that porridge." The helper went back into the kitchen and returned a moment later with a big bowl which he placed on the step.

The white duck had never tasted porridge before and found it a most satisfying meal. He made short work of the food and, quacking his thanks, waddled off for a swim. "Come back tomorrow," called the cook, "and I'll have another bit of something for you!"

"Cheers!" quacked Timothy. Now it was time for a swim, and as the white mallard dabbled peacefully along, a big red boat passed him. People on the boat saw him and began calling and waving to him. Timothy had often seen those big boats cruising up and down the river and he was curious about where they went. So he followed the boat to the Saylor's Famous Thames River Cruises boat landing beside Folly Bridge. The people on the landing saw him and pointed him out to one another. The children laughed, and their parents chuckled. Everyone thought it a splendid joke – a white mallard, what a funny thing!

Timothy frolicked for their amusement and enjoyed the attention. One of the boatmen saw him paddling about and shouted to him. "Ho there, mate! We're just shoving off, come up and join us."

"Thank you," replied Timothy. "I don't mind if I do." He flew on to the landing and waddled up the gangway to the deck of the boat. The passengers laughed when the white mallard took his place on the rail at the prow as the boat cast off. Timothy liked sitting at the very front of the boat and stayed there the entire cruise.

All along the river, people noticed the white mallard. On the shore, or in passing boats, they called to him, and Timothy offered his cheery greeting in reply. "Quack! Quack! Quack!" he called – which was his way of saying, "Hello! Hello! Good to see you!"

He enjoyed the cruise hugely, and had a splendid time. For their part, the boat's crew and captain quite liked having the plucky white duck aboard – he made it seem more of a holiday, somehow. When the ride was over at last, and all the passengers were leaving the boat, the captain told Timothy, "You're welcome aboard my boat any time, my friend. You have a place at the rail whenever we sail. You just come along any time you please."

Timothy thanked the captain politely, then hopped down the gangway and into the water.

He paddled home slowly, chattering his pleasure to one and all. It had been a fine, fine day indeed. And this was only the beginning.

Timothy's life settled into a pleasant routine: days spent visiting friends at Saylor's and the *Head of the River*, strolling in the meadow and swimming along the Thames. Nights were spent in his box at the boat hire. It was a good life, to be sure, and Timothy accepted it gratefully. Certainly, it couldn't have happened to a nicer duck.

Very soon, there wasn't anyone around Folly Bridge who hadn't heard of the Rare White Mallard living there; Timothy quickly became everyone's friend. The cook and kitchen helpers at the restaurant considered him a special pet. Every day they brought him bowl of porridge, a buttered bap stuffed with lettuce, or some other delicacy. And often, in the afternoons, he took a cruise on the river with his friends in the big red boat.

And that wasn't all. Far from it. The rowing crew of Christ Church College made him their official mascot. Tourists from seventeen different countries took snapshots of him to show their friends back home. Holiday-makers taking tea on Christchurch Meadow offered him treats from their picnic hampers. River boats saluted him when they passed him on the water. Walkers on the tow-path stopped in their tracks and chatted with him. And the punters in Bea and Albert's hired boats wished him good day. Everyone who saw him loved him.

In short, Timothy Mallard was one famous duck.

12

Big News
from Big Sam

The other ducks along the river grew used to seeing people make a fuss over Timothy. And, though they didn't much like it at first, in the end they had to admit that whenever Timothy was around, the food fell freely. That is, people seemed to go out of their way to feed him. Timothy could not begin to eat all that was tossed his way, but the others could. And did.

Little by little, the other ducks realized what a friend they had in the rare white mallard. Soon there wasn't a duck around Folly Bridge that didn't welcome Timothy. Why, he had more friends than feathers.

Fame, wealth, popularity – Timothy Mallard had it all. He could hardly swim ten strokes without attracting a crowd of well-wishers, folk lavishing gifts upon him, people taking his picture. Everywhere he went it was, "Good day,

Timothy!" or "Glad to see you, Tim!" He never lacked for a cheerful greeting or a kind word.

One bright morning, Timothy went for a stroll along the riverbank and met some children who had come to the meadow especially to greet him. As he stood there, passing the time of day with his young friends, he got the funny feeling that someone was watching him. He glanced this way and that, but aside from the usual hustle and bustle on the river he saw no one.

Yet the strange feeling would not go away. He thanked the children for coming to see him, and gently nuzzled their fingers by way of saying goodbye. Then he turned and hopped back into the water, almost colliding with a great big swan.

"Oh! Excuse me, I didn't see you sitting th – " he began, then stopped. The swan was staring at him, and Timothy felt certain he'd seen that selfsame stare somewhere before.

"Well, well," said the swan, "I do believe it's the Famous White Mallard of Folly Bridge. Funny, he doesn't look anything like the skinny little hatchling I remember."

"Big Sam!" Timothy gasped. "Where did you come from?"

"Greetings, youngster. I see you're doing well."

"I'm surviving, Big Sam. Thanks to you."

"Thriving, I should say," remarked the swan. "Just look at you now – if that plumage was any brighter, I'd need sunglasses! Celebrity life agrees with you, my boy."

"You're looking good, too, Big Sam. I'm glad to see you. I've wanted to thank you for helping me. I wouldn't have made it if it hadn't been for you. You're a good friend."

The big swan shrugged off the praise. "Oh, something tells me you would have made out all right. I helped steer you along a bit, that's all."

Timothy fell into place beside the swan. "Where are you going?"

"Up to Osney Lock. It's getting on towards high summer and you know what that means – tourists."

"Yes," agreed Timothy. "It's great!"

"For you, maybe," replied Big Sam. "I remember my first summer, too. Smashing! But," he sighed, "when you've been around as long as I have, the glamour wears a bit thin. Now I prefer a quiet canal somewhere away from all the rush and riot – especially *this* summer."

"What's so special about this summer, Big Sam?"

"Haven't you heard?" wondered the swan.

"No, I don't suppose anyone has heard the news yet."

"What news is that?" Timothy nudged closer to hear better.

"This summer is going to be a dry one," Big Sam announced.

"Dry one?"

"No rain all summer long. In short, a drought. That means more tourists, more boats, more river traffic. Humans! Give them a stretch of dry weather and they take to the water in boats. That's why I'm off to Osney Lock; it's quieter there."

"Well, I'm staying right here," declared Timothy. "I wouldn't want to miss any of the fun."

The big swan nodded slowly. "Speaking of missing things," he said, gazing intently at the white mallard. "What about your family? Have you been missing them?"

At those words, Timothy felt his heart sink. Until Big Sam mentioned his family, the white mallard had not missed them at all. He had long ago grown used to being on his own. He had not thought about his mother and father and brothers for a very long time. Nevertheless, the ache in his heart told him he had not forgotten them – not at all.

"No!" Timothy said crossly. "I haven't missed

73

them. Anyway, I don't need them any more – I'm grown up now. I can take care of myself."

"Oh, it wasn't you I was worried about," said the swan. "Maybe it's *them* that need help now. But I don't suppose it's any of my business." Big Sam turned and began paddling away.

"Goodbye, Big Sam!" called Timothy. "Good of you to stop by."

"I'm never very far away," replied the swan. He curled his long neck and continued on his way up the river. "I'll be seeing you, my boy!"

Timothy watched him go. "What a strange swan," he murmured. It is true that good weather brings people to the water. The river would be busy – but what of that? The more the merrier. The more people and boats, the more fun and food and friends. "It's going to be a wonderful summer!" cried Timothy. "I wouldn't miss it for the world." He paused and added, "And I won't miss my wicked brothers, either!"

At once, he swam back to the boat hire, passing other ducks who called after him cheerfully. He returned their greetings, but his heart wasn't in it. The mere mention of his family had made him unhappy, and he didn't like it. He wanted only to be happy, and now Big Sam had ruined that by reminding him of his family.

"Nosey swan!" Timothy muttered to himself. "I *don't* miss them. After what my brothers did to me, I never want to see them again!"

The rare white mallard took his place at the end of the jetty and tried to forget his mean brothers. But the more he tried to forget them, the more he could think of nothing else and the angrier he became. "I don't *want* to remember them," he muttered. "I don't want anything to do with them! This is going to be a wonderful summer – a summer to remember. I won't let them ruin it."

Oh yes, it would be a summer to remember. But not the way Timothy expected.

13

The Long, Hot Summer

A few days later, a strange, bright, shining object appeared in the sky: it was the sun. Amazing – but true! Someone who had once been to Spain confirmed the sighting, and everyone agreed it was a marvel, a genuine phenomenon.

Each day dawned fresh and bright, with clear, blue skies and not a cloud to be seen anywhere. People walked around without umbrellas and did not get wet! Sometimes a small cloud or two came in the evening, but it did not rain. The weather stayed warm and dry all the time. The whole countryside was astonished, flabbergasted. Think of it: sun and warmth . . . in the heart of England . . . all summer long! Unbelievable!

And just as Big Sam had predicted, people took to the water in boats. Rickety rowing-boats, narrow canal boats, sleek sailing-boats, flat-bottomed punts, luxury double-decked cruisers, and hulky houseboats – anything that would float. They all passed by the *Head of the River* and stopped for lunch on the terrace. Every day Christchurch Meadow filled with sunbathers, picnickers and tea-takers. The rowing crews rowed away from dawn to dusk. The boat hire's boats were hired from the moment they opened the doors in the morning until they locked away the last oar at night. Bea and Albert both said that they had never in all their years seen such a busy summer. The river fairly hummed.

The weeks drifted by like the lazy river itself: slow and steady, with scarcely a ripple of difference to tell one splendid day from the next. But alas, further up-river things were not so pleasant. The creatures of Riverbank were not enjoying the fine weather at all. For, as the long, hot summer dragged on, the water in the canal began to dry up.

The residents of Riverbank began to worry. "If this continues," they told one another, "it will be the end of us."

Sadly, that was true. Every Riverbank creature depended on the small canal in one way or another. Without it, they would die.

Bodger Badger, Lord Mayor of Riverbank, tried to calm them with soothing words. "Friends, citizens, voters," he said, "relax. No need to go getting all worked up over this. Enjoy the sun. If you don't mind my saying so, you all could use a good tan." He laughed out loud to show how confident he was. "Relax, there's nothing to worry about."

But no one was convinced. Every day the sun rose up, and the water level of the canal went down. Just a little. But enough for everyone to notice.

The ducks suffered most. They depended on the water for their food. As the canal began to dry up, food ran short and the ducks went hungry.

It was bad for all the ducks, but worse for Malcolm and Meryl Mallard. They had eight children at home – that made eight hungry bills to feed. Timothy's brothers, too lazy or too content, still lived at home with their parents, and expected to be fed.

Why, it nearly drove their mother crazy, finding food for them. Every day she'd take them up and down the canal, scouring the banks and shallows for any stray scrap. There was little enough to be found. And there were other ducks out searching for meals, too. By midsummer things were looking pretty grim at the Malcolm Mallard nest.

"You've got to do something, Malcolm," said

Meryl Mallard. "It's getting so that I can't find a bite to eat."

"Am I a rain-maker, Meryl? What do you want me to do?"

"You could speak to our sons, at least," she said. "I'm running myself ragged trying to keep them in watercress. Those overgrown egglings should have left the nest long ago."

"The lads? Oh, the lads are all right, love," Malcolm told her. "They're good boys."

"Good and hungry – it seems to me. I can't keep this up much longer, Malcolm. Something will have to be done."

But what *could* be done? Could Malcolm make the duckweed grow? Could he fill the canal with water? Could he make the rain fall?

No. There was nothing to be done. Each day the family paddled along the canal searching for a scrap here, a mouthful there, watching the water dry up a little more. Each day they had to go a little further to find something to eat.

One day the search took them all the way to Osney Lock, where some of Riverbank's creatures had gathered to wait out the dry spell. And, as soon as the other ducks saw them, they puffed up their feathers and began hissing. "Shove off! Free-loaders! Go on, get away!"

"But we're hungry," said Meryl Mallard, "and we've come all this way."

"And you can go right back again. We don't need your lot around here – there's little enough for us as it is. Move on!"

"Let's go, lads," said Malcolm. "I can see we're not welcome here."

They turned round and began the long swim home again. The last duck in line, Brother Number Eight, heard someone call out to him. "You there! Mallard! Wait a moment."

Brother Number Eight turned and saw a big swan behind him. "We're leaving, don't worry," he said, wondering where the swan had come from. He hadn't heard anyone swim up behind him.

"Are you Malcolm's brood?" the big swan asked.

"Maybe," Number Eight answered slyly. "What's it to you?"

"It's nothing to me," answered the strange swan. "I only thought it might be something to you."

"What's that, then?"

"You are hungry – " began the swan.

"So what!" sneered the duck. "Is that a crime?"

"Not at all," replied the swan calmly. "I only find it a bit odd. I mean, here you are, begging for food, while your brother has more food than he can eat in a hundred years."

"My brother? Which brother is that?"

"The white one," replied the big swan. "Timothy, by name."

"I don't know what you're talking about."

"You *are* Malcolm Mallard's brood, aren't you?"

"And just who are you?" Brother Number Eight demanded.

"They call me Big Sam," the swan told him. "Your brother Timothy is thriving. He is a celebrity."

"What makes you think he's *my* brother?" asked the duck suspiciously. "I don't know anything about anyone named Timothy."

"Sorry," sniffed the swan, "I thought you'd be interested to know how he's getting on. I see I was wrong." Big Sam stretched his wings and made ready to fly.

"Hey! Wait a second! Where'd you say this Timothy was staying?"

"At Folly Bridge," answered Big Sam as he flapped away. "Ask anyone – they'll tell you. He's very famous."

14

One Who Dared

All the long, hungry way home Brother Number Eight – an earnest duck named Oscar – thought about what Big Sam had told him. Especially the part about "more food than he can eat in a hundred years". By the time he reached the nest, he had decided to go and see for himself if what the mysterious swan said was true.

Oscar – being the last among his brothers since Timothy had gone – did not say anything about his plan. He knew the others would make fun of him. He also knew that they'd try to discourage him. After all, they'd run Timothy off in the first place – that was the guilty secret they all shared. And they wouldn't take kindly to the idea of someone going to find him.

So Number Eight kept his news to himself and, next morning, before any of the others were awake and stirring, he set off for Folly Bridge. He didn't know where it was exactly, or how far, but he struck off just the same.

The morning was warm and bright; it would be another long, hot day. The young duck swam down-river in search of Folly Bridge. As he paddled along, he thought about Timothy for the first time in a very long time. He wondered how the duckling had survived, and how he had come to be famous. As he thought more about him, Oscar realized he missed Timothy. Yes, and before very long he was very, very sorry for the wicked trick they had all played on the little white fellow.

"He probably won't even speak to me," thought the duck. "Nor do I blame him. I wouldn't speak to any of us either, after what we did to him." Still, Oscar did not turn back. If there was even the slightest chance that what Big Sam said was true, he had to see it through. He was too hungry to do anything else.

After swimming a fair distance, Oscar saw a bridge up ahead and swam to it. "Is this Folly Bridge?" he asked a frog sitting on the bank underneath it.

"Don't think much of this heat!" said the frog. "Don't think much of it at all. What's that you say? Hot? I'll say it's hot."

"Yes," agreed Oscar, "it is hot. But I'm looking for Folly Bridge."

"Folly? Folly?" croaked the frog. "Well, this isn't it, is it? Of course not. You want the Folly – that's down-river from here, isn't it? Everyone knows that."

"I'll just keep going as I am, shall I?" asked the duck. "And I'll get to it eventually – is that right?"

But the frog closed his eyes and would say no more. Oscar continued on, no more certain than before. And soon he noticed that the grassy riverbank was gone – everything was concrete and stone now. The river was wider, too, and boats were thick on the water. He could hardly swim for being dashed this way and that by the wash and chop.

But he kept close to the stone bank and drifted along, hardly daring to think that what Big Sam had told him might be true. But he did dare, and he hoped with all his might that maybe . . . just maybe . . . Oh, that *maybe* was too much to hope for. The young duck swallowed hard and swam on.

85

15

A Jolt from the Past

Timothy, fresh from a nap on the jetty, was thinking about his afternoon's errands. He had lately become very busy; for, as the summer grew longer and drier, many more ducks had come to Folly Bridge and the *Head of the River* to beg for food. Timothy helped them all he could, and he was a very good help: whenever the white mallard appeared, people opened their lunch bags and picnic hampers and the food showered down around him.

Timothy shared his good fortune with the others. Indeed, but for him many others would have starved. As the most famous duck around, it was up to him to care for the less celebrated. He took his duty seriously, and spent a lot of time thinking about how best to help all the needy waterfowl.

He was thinking about this very thing as he sat

on the jetty of the busy boat hire, when he saw a strange duck swimming towards him. "Another hungry mouth to feed," he sighed. But as the duck came closer Timothy felt a funny quivery flutter in his stomach. "I know this duck, I think. But how? I'm sure I've never seen him before. And yet . . ." He stared hard at the strange duck, who seemed to become more familiar the closer he swam.

Could it be? . . . Was it? . . . No, it couldn't be!

It was!

"It's my brother!" gasped Timothy. "Oh, no!" What a jolt! And so unexpected he didn't know what to do. "No time to think – here he comes!" Timothy gulped.

"Good day to you," said the duck, as he swam to the jetty where Timothy sat.

"Hello," replied Timothy, not letting on that he knew his visitor. "I haven't seen you around before. What brings you here?"

"I heard there was a famous white duck at Folly Bridge and decided to come and see for myself." Brother Number Eight, looked closely at the white duck. "You are Timothy Mallard, aren't you?"

"That's me," Timothy told him. "Who are you?"

"I'm Oscar – Malcolm Mallard's boy," answered the duck slowly, and added, "I'm your brother. Don't you recognize me?"

Timothy didn't answer. He didn't know what answer to make. Instead he said, "Are you hungry?"

"Yes," admitted Oscar. "It was quite a long trip. I could use a bite to eat."

"Then come with me," Timothy said. He splashed into the water and led his brother a little way down-river to Christchurch Meadow. Along the way, other ducks saw Timothy and hurried to join him, so that by the time they reached the meadow a whole flock of noisy waterfowl followed.

"Is it always this crowded?" wondered Oscar. He was used to Riverbank, where things were quieter.

"They come from all over for the food," Timothy told him. "Watch this."

Timothy hopped up on the bank and began waddling among the picnickers and tea-takers. Instantly, the children saw him and began breaking off bits of their biscuits and sandwiches, and tossing them to the famous white mallard. Just like magic, the hampers and bags opened and the food appeared – whereupon Timothy

promptly turned around and jumped back into the river.

The people followed him, of course, and showered the food into the river. Now the other ducks could get at it and Timothy swam back and forth along the bank, keeping the people entertained while the hungry ducks fed.

"What do you think of that?" Timothy asked when he returned to his brother.

"Shhplendid!" said Oscar, whose mouth was full of ginger cake. "I haven't eaten so well in months. Wait till I tell the others!"

"Others?"

"My brothers – I mean, *our* brothers; and mother and father. You must remember them, Timothy."

Timothy did remember, of course. But he pretended not to. He had said he never wanted to see his brothers again, and he meant it. But now that he had one of them standing right there in front of him, he wasn't so sure.

Oscar continued, "We're all hungry these days. And here you have plenty. I can't wait to tell them!"

"Just as I thought," said Timothy. "You're a free-loader. All you want from me is a free meal."

"Oh, no," protested Oscar quickly. "It isn't like that at all. We miss you, Timothy."

"Hmph!" sniffed Timothy, and turned away.

"Please, Timothy. How can I prove it to you?"

"You can't expect me to help you there. You'll have to think of something on your own."

"I will," said Oscar. "And when I do, I'll be back!"

With that, Brother Number Eight turned right around and started for home. Timothy watched him go. He thought about calling Oscar back, but kept his bill clamped firmly shut. "Let him go and good riddance," he thought to himself. "I don't want anything to do with any of them."

16

Alive and Thriving

Oscar raced back to the canal as fast as he could go, and arrived at sunset. He chugged home exhausted from the journey, but excited to share his news. "Hey! Hey!" he quacked as he flopped into the nest. "You'll never guess who I saw today!"

"Where have you been, Oscar?" demanded his mother. "I've been worried sick about you all day."

"I've been to Folly Bridge," the young duck replied.

"Folly Bridge?" wondered Malcolm. "Where's that, then?"

"Down-river – quite a long way from here. But – "

"What'd you want to go there for?" asked Brother Number One.

"That's not important right now," said Oscar. "I saw – "

"Not important?" said his father. "Your mum and me half out of our wits over you and you say it's not important? Why, I ought to give you a good thrashing."

"Now, Malcolm," said Mrs Mallard. "Don't be hard on the boy. He's back safe and sound. I'm sure he must have had a good reason to run away."

"But I didn't run away," Oscar insisted. "I went to see Timothy!"

"What?" asked his mother. "What?" asked his father. "What?" asked Brothers One to Seven. "What did you say?"

"I've been to see Timothy – and I have seen him."

"Timothy? Our little lost Timothy?" Meryl Mallard started to cry. "Alive?"

"Alive and thriving!" announced Oscar. "What's more, he's famous!"

"Go on," said his brothers. "Whitey? Famous?"

"And rich!" Number Eight informed them. "He's got more food than he can eat in a hundred years. He's living like a king at Folly Bridge. Ducks come from all over and Timothy makes sure they get fed. He's wonderful!"

"Is he still white?" wondered Malcolm.

"Whiter than ever! He's famous, I tell you."

"Well, well, think of that," mused his mother, tears coming to her eyes. "Alive and thriving. My little Timothy. I'm so happy for him!"

"Fat lot of good it does us," grouched Brother Number One. "Him being all high and mighty like, and us starving here."

"Don't take on so, son," soothed his father. "He's family. We should be glad he didn't end up a cat's dinner."

"Malcolm!" cried Mrs Mallard.

"Well, it's true, isn't it? We all thought he was dead, didn't we? Poor little white thing, lost and all," sniffed Malcolm, dabbing at his eyes with a wing tip. "That's what happens to lost hatchlings."

"He always was a show-off," muttered Number Two. "It would have served him right to get et up."

"That's enough," said the mother duck. "I won't hear another word against our Timothy. We should all be happy for him."

They said no more about it then, but that night, as they settled to sleep in the nest, the brothers began mumbling once more.

"I don't believe it's really him," said Brother Number One.

"Nor do I," said Brother Number Two.

94

"It couldn't be," said Brothers Three to Seven.

"I tell you it *is* Timothy," Oscar insisted. "Come with me tomorrow and I'll show you. What is more, he'll feed us. He really does have enough food for all."

The brothers, hungry as they were, did not like to think that Timothy was really alive and thriving. But what if it *were* true? What then? They didn't like to think about that either.

Not one of them slept that night; they had very guilty consciences. None of the brothers could stop thinking about the cruel trick they'd played on Timothy, and how, now that he was famous, he would take his revenge. Oh, yes, he would.

17

Sweet Revenge

Timothy did not sleep well that night, either. He fluffed and re-fluffed his feathers, and tucked his bill under first one wing, and then the other. He tossed; he turned. He told himself it was too warm to sleep. Yes, it was warm. But that was not why he couldn't sleep.

He couldn't sleep because he was angry. He was angry with his brothers and he was angry with himself. "I behaved very badly," Timothy told himself. "Very, very badly."

Then he would think: "I didn't ask Oscar to come here. He should have stayed away."

But then he would think: "He is my brother, and I treated him badly." And he would feel ashamed, until he remembered how badly his brothers had treated him.

He remembered bad old Boris, and felt again those wicked sharp claws on his back. He remembered the horrible, helpless feeling of being trapped and tortured by that mean cat.

And Timothy remembered Spike. He felt again those nasty teeth tight on his leg, and the awful racing of his small heart in terror as that cold monster pulled him down into the dark depths. He remembered struggling under water, fighting for his life.

All this Timothy remembered, and more: the dreadful fear of being lost, the grief of missing his family, and the long, lonely nights when he cried himself to sleep. When he remembered these things, he wanted nothing more than to be with his family again and have everything just as it was before – all the bad memories of the past forgotten.

But he could not forget. And when he thought of how his brothers had caused him so much pain, he grew angry once more. "They tricked me most cruelly. I might have been killed. They deserve what happens to them now."

Strangely, Timothy also remembered what Big Sam had told him: *Maybe it's them that need help now.* And he thought, "Maybe this is why I've been given so much – to help my family." Then he'd think, "But what did they ever do for me, except try to hurt me?"

This went on all night; he thrashed first this way, then the other. And by morning he was no better off for all his thrashing about. His heart was as heavy as a boatyard brick. One part of him wanted just to be happy, and for everything to be the way it was before. The other part wanted revenge.

Revenge, sweet and delicious. How good it would be to see his cruel brothers put in their place at last. What would he do? What would be best? He could introduce them to Bad Boris – that would fix them. Or he could steer them into the snapping jaws of Spike the Pike and see what they thought of that! Or perhaps slow starvation – nothing would be too bad for those low-down schemers.

So many possibilities; so many ways to get even. Timothy spent the entire morning thinking up ways to take his revenge. He told himself that making his no-good nasty brothers suffer as he had suffered was what he wanted most. And he thought that getting what he wanted would make him happy again. But the more he thought about getting even, the more beastly he felt about it.

In the end, however, he concluded that feeling good wasn't the important thing. He wanted revenge for the evil trick played on him, and revenge he would have. "If I ever see those dastardly ducks again," he promised himself, "I will make certain that they get just what they deserve."

As it happened, Timothy got his chance much sooner than he expected. The morning passed, and the crowds began to gather along the river. The white mallard decided to make the rounds and get a bite to eat for himself, and the other ducks flocked about.

He rose and walked to the end of the jetty, fluffed his feathers and beat his wings. He was flapping away when he heard someone quack his name. "Timothy! Halloo, Timothy!"

He looked out on the river and saw Oscar stroking steadily towards him. His brother had returned! Timothy's first thought was to fly to meet Oscar and put his wings around him in welcome.

But then he looked and saw that behind his brother came the rest: brothers one, two, three, four, five, six and seven. He saw them and remembered his revenge. Timothy's heart fell like a lump to his feet. "Steady, old boy," he told himself. "It has to be done. They must be taught a lesson they will never forget."

The eight ducks swam up to the boat hire jetty

where Timothy waited. Oscar, leading the rest, spoke first. "Please, don't get angry," he quacked. "I just had to come back. I brought the rest of your brothers with me. When I told them about you, they had to see you for themselves. So here we are."

Timothy puffed out his chest importantly and glared at the ducks before him. "A passel of panhandlers!" he declared. "I ought to send you packing, the lot of you!"

The brothers cringed. Oh, now surely Timothy would punish them for what they had done. They all knew they had it coming, but they couldn't face it. All eight hung their heads so low their bills almost touched the water.

"This is going to be easier than I thought," muttered Timothy to himself. "Now I'll make them suffer like I suffered. I'll have my revenge at last!"

But what would it be? Boris? Spike? A rowing accident? Slow starvation?

The brothers huddled fearfully together. They quaked and shivered with fear. They were so hungry, and so tired. And so afraid. Why, oh why, had they come? "Please, Timothy," cried Oscar, "have pity on us. We didn't know what else to do."

The famous white mallard of Folly Bridge looked down upon his forlorn family. How miserable they were. How hungry and bedraggled they looked. How silly this all was. And how foolish he felt, lording it over them. The whole thing was absurd. Nevertheless, he had to see it through. They had to be taught a lesson.

Timothy drew a deep, determined breath . . .

"Welcome!" he gasped at last. He couldn't do it – he couldn't punish his own family. "Welcome, brothers. I'm glad you have come. Are you hungry? I will get you something to eat."

The seven brothers looked at one another in astonishment. "It's a trick!" whispered Brother Number One.

"I don't think so," said Oscar. "I'm sure he means it."

"It's got to be a trick – and we deserve it," argued Brother Number Two.

"After what we did to him, who can blame him?" put in Brother Number Three. "We treated him terribly."

"It was an awful thing to do," said Brother Number Four.

"Wicked," agreed Brother Number Five. "We were wrong to do it."

"Well, he will surely get even now," pointed out Brother Number Six. "We're in for it."

"He has us right where he wants us," added Brother Number Seven. "We're helpless."

The brothers all looked unhappily at one another, and then at Timothy standing over them. Tears filled their eyes. "We're sorry, Timothy," they all wailed. "We're so sorry for the awful thing we did to you. Please, don't hurt us."

"Don't be afraid." Timothy said with a smile, "I'm not going to hurt you. I forgive you. I never hated you, and I am not going to start now."

"See?" quacked Oscar happily to the others, "I told you he would help us. When I saw how he helped the others, I knew he wouldn't turn us away."

"Turn away my own family? Never!" cried Timothy. He dived into the midst of them and they all began flapping their wings and slapping one another happily, splashing and quacking and laughing. In that moment, all the hurt and grief of the past was forgotten.

Forgiving them was much more satisfying than punishing them. Peace was so much sweeter than revenge. Timothy's heavy heart rose in happiness. The rare white mallard thought he had never felt better.

18

A Prince among Ducks

The nine ducks spent a happy day on the river. Timothy fed his brothers and showed them all around. They ate lunch at the *Head of the River*, had a snack at the boatyard, swam among the punters for fun, and took tea on the meadow.

"Tell me, how are Mum and Dad?" asked Timothy, as they swam back to the jetty. It was late; the moon had risen long ago, but Timothy wasn't tired – there was still so much catching up to do.

"Mum and Dad are well enough," replied Oscar. "It's been a hard summer for them, of course. But when they heard you were alive they were so happy. Mum cried; Dad, too. They love you very much, Timothy." Oscar paused and looked at his brothers. "We all do."

"Take me to them," Timothy said.

"Now?" asked Oscar. "You want to go now? But it's so far. We'd have to swim all night."

"I must see them at once. Come on, let's go."

Timothy and his brothers set off then and there. Oscar led the way, and they swam back along the winding river – past the stone banks and houses, past the steel bridge, past the place where the river and canal divide, and along the riverbank to where the tall rushes grew. It took them all night.

The sun was coming up when they arrived. Timothy could see that the water was well down. And much of what used to be wet and green was now brown and dry. The long, hot summer had taken its toll. But when they came to the mallard nest in the long reeds, the place looked exactly the same as he remembered it. Timothy shouted for joy.

His cry roused his parents, who woke up and poked their heads through the reeds, and saw, swimming towards them, their long lost son.

"Timothy!" cried his mother.

"Son, is it really you?" quacked his father.

Timothy flew to meet them. His parents fell upon him, hugging him, nuzzling him, stroking him with their wings. Oh, it was a wonderful reunion. The brothers looked on, quacking happily and splashing one another and raising an early-morning ruckus on the river.

"You've come back," gasped his mother. "Look how you've grown. How handsome you are!"

"We hear you're doing well, son," said his father. "Your old mum and dad are proud of you."

"I missed you so much," said Timothy. "I never dreamed I'd see you again."

Then Timothy began to tell them all that had happened to him since he became lost. He told of his futile search, his struggle with Boris, meeting the humpy-backed monster, and his narrow escape from Spike. He described his miraculous rescue by Big Sam, being adopted by Bea and Albert, becoming famous, and all the rest.

Mother and father mallard listened to every word, marvelling at his courage and cleverness. The brothers listened, too, becoming more ashamed than ever of their thoughtless cruelty to him. They began apologizing to him all over again.

"We're so sorry, Timothy. Can you ever forgive us?" they wailed.

"But I have already forgiven you," Timothy told them. "Maybe you meant me harm, but a very great good has come of it. How else would I be able to save you now?"

"Save us?" they asked warily. "What do you mean?" They could hardly believe Timothy meant what he said about forgiving them. They still expected to be punished in some way.

"Listen," Timothy said, "if you had not done what you did, I would never have become lost. If I had not become lost, I would never have met Big Sam, who led me to Folly Bridge and the *Head of the River*. If you hadn't tricked me, I would have stayed here and we would all be starving now. It was bad being lost, but starving is much worse."

"He's right about that," everyone agreed.

"Listen," the white duck said earnestly, "this dry spell is far from over – there are many dry days yet to come. If you stay here you will surely starve. You must come back with me to Folly Bridge. That is my place; it's where I belong. I have food enough for all; I can take care of you there. We will all be happy."

Timothy Mallard took his mother and father and Brothers One to Eight back to the boat hire at Folly Bridge. There, as Timothy had promised, they had plenty to eat and water enough to keep them cool and wet for the rest of the long, hot

summer. A happier little flock there surely never was.

Indeed, the mallard family can still be seen paddling along the river, dodging cruise boats, or waddling at the edge of Christchurch Meadow. And the Famous White Mallard of Folly Bridge is still celebrated for his beautiful plumage and friendly way with people. But no one sings his praises more highly than his eight brothers, who are often heard to remark to passing strangers, "That is our brother, Timothy. He is a prince among ducks. Let me tell you what he did . . ."

This is how the tale of one duck's generous and forgiving heart has spread all along the riverbank – and beyond.

Saylor's River Cruises

Folly Bridge

River

Head of the River

To Christchurch Meadow

To Oxpens Bridge